Desdemona and the Eggs

Written and Illustrated by Patty Gannon

AuthorHouse™
1663 Liberty Drive
Bloomington, IN 47403
www.authorhouse.com
Phone: 1-800-839-8640

First published by AuthorHouse 3/2/2011

ISBN: 978-1-4567-1581-6 (sc)
Library of Congress Control Number: 2010918712

Printed in the United States of America

This book is printed on acid-free paper.

DESDEMONA

In memory of my mother, who taught me that
my greatest glory is not in never failing, but
getting up every time I do. And to my son Ben,
who outgrew my lap, but never my heart.

Desdemona lives at the bottom of an old oak tree with her mother.

She loves to jump rope. She figures if she could ever jump 100 times she would certainly go around the world. Needless to say, her world is very small.

Desdemona loves to garden. She loves the way the sunflower seeds feel under her feet and the way they go crunch, crunch, crunch in her mouth.

FRESH EGGS

And she loves the days she goes to the egg farm with her mother...

because Miss Isabelle gives Desdemona warm cookies right out of the oven...

and “Big Daddy” takes her for tractor rides.

HAPPY
BIRTHDAY

But Desdemona's birthday is by far her very most favoritest day of all in the whole wide world. Blowing out the candles and making the wish is the very best part, because Desdemona's wishes - always - come true. And this year, she wishes to be grown up.

WIZARD of OZ
The Giving Tree
Matilda
FERDINAND

One night when Mother is reading her a bedtime story, she says, "Desdemona, you're getting so grown up I'm going to let you go to the egg farm all by yourself tomorrow." The little mouse is so excited she can hardly get to sleep.

Desdemona gets up very early the next morning, runs out the door to the egg farm, barely saying goodbye to her mother. When she gets so far away and can no longer see her house, she gets...

so scared! She gets the *"what ifs."* "What if I get lost? What if there is a snake in the grass? WHAT IF THE WOLF WANTS TO EAT ME FOR LUNCH?" And with that last thought, Desdemona becomes...

frozen in the clutches of her own fear! Her world is way too big!

All Desdemona can do is turn and face the light and take in a very deep breath. Inside that breath she hears her Mother's voice, "Desdemona, you know you are growing up when you find the courage and strength to face your fear." Desdemona takes another deep breath...

and runs as fast as
she can all the way
to the egg farm,

where she gathers up a basketful of the very freshest eggs,

and runs all the way back home.

When she gets home, Desdemona discovers she has broken ALL her eggs! "Geezie Beezie," cries Desdemona, "how am I going to tell my mom?"

She is so sad as she walks inside her house. Mother, seeing the empty basket, gives her a big hug and says, "They're — JUST EGGS — Desdemona. You can go back tomorrow and get some more. When you get back, we will make us an extra-rich double dark chocolate cake." Desdemona takes another deep breath. She is not so sure she likes all her wishes coming true. Maybe she could wait to be grown up.

Desdemona gets up early the next morning to go to the egg farm again. This time, Mother sees her off with a big hug and encouraging words.

As she's walking down the road, Desdemona takes lots of deep breaths and only looks back once.

Before she knows it, she is gathering up another basketful of the very freshest eggs and is saying goodbye to Miss Isabelle.

Desdemona makes it home with all her eggs just in time to help Mother bake the extra-rich double dark chocolate cake. After eating a very big piece of cake, Desdemona decides she needs some quiet time. She will make magic with color.

Desmond

As she's coloring, Desdemona thinks to herself, "You know, when I really, REALLY, R—E—E——ALLY grow up, I'm going to color my story."

DESDEMONA and the EGGS

AND she does!!!